THE TRIAL OF
MANKIND

VINCENT STACEY DIXON

PAGE PUBLISHING, INC.
New York, NY

First originally published by Page Publishing, Inc. 2017

ISBN 978-1-68348-717-3 (Paperback)
ISBN 978-1-68348-718-0 (Digital)

Printed in the United States of America

Character Names

Narrator .... Jackson Pendrift (as a man)

Father .... Elroy Pendrift

Boy .... Jackson Pendrift (as a young boy)

The Bear .... Beau Le Fay

The Chimpanzee .... Turpan

The Crow (in the tower) .... Mercantz

The Lion Judge .... Mordecai

The King Cobra .... Kazarack

The Eagle .... Cloud Rider

The Dog .... General

The Fox .... Chesterfield Farthingsworth III

The Tasmanian Tiger .... The Bangleman

The King of Parrots .... Tripidium

The Queen of Hyenas .... Nadonia

The Queen of Felines .... Kalayja

The Crocodile .... Grozohn

The Mother .... Inger Pendrift

The Mouse .... Portriva

The Mandrill .... Kamoru

DEDICATION

First and foremost I want to thank God for watching me go to the brink of utter damnation, hearing my cry for mercy and answering my prayers. I realize now that back then I may have lost his favor... but never his grace...AMEN. I want to thank my mother and father, who recognized that I was different and didn't seek to change me but taught me how to fit in and survive. Thank you to all my family and friends who supported me through the years no matter what my endeavor was. Last, but certainly not least I am proud to thank the one person who not only saw more in me than anyone else (including myself), but went the extra mile by feeding me a steady supply of ink and paper and inspiration. We played over 3,000 games of scrabble to further increase my vocabulary. She was always ready with a "when? Where? Why? How?" Or "what do you see?" To my lovely wife Consuello (Connie) I say thank you for the love and hard work you put into bringing this story to life. May God bless you all...AMEN!

Way down yonder where the woods are black, where the trees are tall and the leaves are stacked, insects fluttering in the air and creepers crawling underneath, trying to find a place to hide or looking for something to eat. Flora and fauna thrive in unity as flowers bloom in great quantities. Here live animals in coexistence all over the place—far, far from the human race. It is there where all is as nature intended and springtime unfolds within it. Where mammals cry out at the joy of giving birth and the circle of life continues on earth. In the nests, eggs cracking open as they begin to hatch. That's where my papa sent me hunting for food to catch. He said, "Don't come back till you can feed this family, boy! You can take my rifle, but don't forget it ain't a toy. This here is a Winchester Special with a pop-up sight. Make sure you lean a little to the left when you aim because the tip is bent a little to the right." Then he cradled his suspenders with a great big smile and flashed his teeth speaking in that deep southern style, saying, "Go ahead, boy, and stay out there for a while." So with all the enthusiasm of a child on Christmas morn, I set out to prove my manhood was born.

As the sunlight danced below the trees, I tiptoed through the woods with a bend in my knees, confident and proud of the hunter I will be. I turned around just in time to see a great big old bear looking back at me.

He said, "Hey there, boy, what you gonna do with that gun? You best be careful you might hurt someone. Walking through these woods like you own the land holding that rifle as if you about to strike. If I didn't know any better, I'd say you were hunting, and around here that will get you into a fight."

The bear was massive and intimidating in size. I could not hide the panic that was posing in my eyes. With a

tremble in my voice and my lips
weighing a ton, I fearfully
said as I raised the gun,
"Well, mister, bear that's
what I aims to do, and
from where I'm standing, it
could be you. I came to these woods
to hunt for my family. I will take you down. You
must understand me."

"Now hold on, boy, don't you move so fast. I
got razor-sharp claws that will cut you like glass.
There's a snake over your head that will bite before
you blink, and a poisonous spider on your ankle.
Now it's time for you to think. You walk into these
woods with your foolish man pride killing
our offspring and taking our hides. Why
can't you just go and leave us alone?
Remember, you too are merely flesh
and bone. Understand one thing,
boy: In God, you may trust, but
that same God gave ani-

mals fur, it belongs to us! We don't go around busting up your home and taking everything we see. Animals have learned to respect man's boundaries. The creatures in these woods have decided to unite. If you hunt us by day, we'll stalk you by night. Your kind is destroying our world with your quest for this master plan. There are those who are calling for the extinction of man!" As I looked around the dense green foliage, through deep branched trees, I perceived images forming between the leaves. They were all sorts of animals staring back at me. Suddenly, a chimpanzee slid down from a vine. He quickly stopped his movement as his eyes met mine. I could tell by his expression this was no game. Something was terribly wrong, and I was being made the blame. I clearly felt my life was in danger as he snatched the rifle from my hand, and in a muffled voice, he said, "Choose your words wisely, my son, to continue the existence of man."

The chimpanzee and the bear led me deep into the woods to an abandoned fort. I heard a voice yell out from the tower above me, "There's a human coming in! Report! Report!" We crossed a drawbridge over a babbling brook below, water so crystal clear the sun gave it an aqua blue glow. We kept on walking down a long dirt road until we passed a huge iron gate. There I saw antelopes, gazelles, kangaroos, and even diamond back snakes. We continued walking down a lengthy gray hall toward two beautiful bronze doors. When they slowly began to creak open (*ROAR!*), I was surprised by a mighty lion's roar. Then I saw him and what looked like a jury and realized how much this place resembled a court. Never in my life had I seen such a thing: all of a hunter's prey sitting in a parliamentary ring. Many of the animals stared at me with disgust, so I lowered my head and covered my eyes. I thought to myself, *What would papa think of me right now?* As I fought back the urge to cry.

The chimpanzee touched my shoulder as he pointed down the aisle toward my designated seat, but the old bear had to give me a nudge; I just couldn't move my feet. My heart began to race as I understood my place before the counsel of all the creatures in the world. I was there to take the stand as a sole voice for the human clan to halt the eradication of man.

CHAPTER II

All were chattering with anticipation as the majestic lion looked over the animal crowd. His mane stood high upon his neck as he began to roar out loud. (*ROAR!*)

His earth-shattering voice so loud that it shook the walls and demanded silence from one and all.

"Hear ye, hear ye, court is now in session. We are here to discuss man's transgressions. Is there anyone among us willing to take the task at hand, and counsel on his behalf, in the defense of man?" The air became filled with grunts and growls, hoots and peeps, snarls and howls.

"I will!" someone hissed. "I will!" the King Cobra said. "Though if it were left up to me alone, I'd rather see you dead. Yet I have long desired to get in man's head."

"Do you accept his counsel?" The first question directed to me. "After all, it is your trial. You have a right to disagree."

"I decline!" I said, trying to sound like a man in everyone's eyes. "I believe the King Cobra would only hasten man's demise, not to mention what he just said, about if it were his choice alone man would be dead."

"Is there anyone else willing to offer voice?" the Lion said.

"And if no one else answers" the snake sizzled, "you'll have no choice." The air again, became filled with all kinds of animal noises—roars of hatred, screams for mercy—but I managed to maintain my poise.

All the animals seemed quite upset. There were debates going on in every seat. Birds squeaking, squawking, and quacking; quadrupeds stomping their feet. There was even a full-blown fight between a ferret and a parakeet. With a strong gust of wind from his mighty wings, the King of Eagles did land. "I'll be his voice. I'll fight against the extinction of man. For hundreds of years, he has honored my kind, tried to learn about us, and helped us survive. It is my duty and a pleasure to stand at his side."

"I will also speak for him" the King of Canines jumped in. "For it is no secret to all that we are man's best friend. We willingly live with him, play with him. We even share his food. Which sometimes include some of you. We will now stand in his defense. He has our gratitude."

"I agree and accept their counsel!" I blurted out of turn. "I know they will help me in this matter of great concern." The lion nodded his head and said, "You will have one hour to form a plan. Prosecution stand ready! For the trial of man!"

CHAPTER III

When the sun began to hide and the moonlight started to peek, animals for and against man shuffled to take their seats. So much excitement being poured into this trial. So many creatures believing man's been due this for a while. As I waited for the events to unfold, the Queen of Koalas came to me, and this is what I was told: "The Bald Eagle would lead my defense." I thought with his strategic mind and emboldened stature, it only makes sense. I was informed that he will have much help from many of the other animals to prepare strategies before the proceedings commence.

Next, I talked with the dog, eagle, and the bear also getting good advice from the Queen of Hares. We decided to point out man's attributes, and how he has grown from his savage youth: his fights against pollution and disease in the seas and oceans, all of his achievements in veterinarian medicines and other curable potions. We know they'll talk about man's terribly vicious wars and how his very existence has closed many animals' life doors. How he hunts just for the sport of it all, and the barbaric ritual of stuffed heads on the wall.

They'll talk about his carelessness with chemical spills, forcing animals to do things totally against their will. Insidious testing on animals to see the effects, before trying it on themselves. Taxidermist, who turn them into ornaments or book ends on shelves. We will counter with conservation, preservation, and wildlife reserves. (They'll bring up the four-wheeled monsters that leave them dead on the curves). The time for planning has gone by quickly, and I must admit that I still felt a little sickly. Still our thoughts were sound and clear. Now the hour is over and the time is near. I will soon speak for all mankind, and I refuse to show any fear.

CHAPTER IV

The defense staff surrounded me as I was escorted back to court from our chamber. They wanted to make sure I returned without any danger. With a slam of his gavel and a mighty roar, silence covered the crowd. The lion's eyes shifted back and forth, and his huge size made him appear confident and proud. "When you take the stand, state your tribe so that all can be heard out loud. Be ye beast of burden or tiny mouse or mighty bird of prey, all who wish to be heard should prepare what he or she wishes to say. We are here to discuss, with animal honor and trust. Mankind must now rely on our faith. Prosecutor you may begin! Call your first witness to the stand. The trial of mankind can no longer wait."

At this moment, I can hardly breathe—sweaty palms, weakened knees, Oh why? Oh why? Who chose me! I was only an adolescent boy sent to do a man's deed. The smell of papa's musky cologne came wafting through the air. If he were in my shoes right now, he'd shoot them all without a care. But it wasn't papa, it was me, and from what I was hearing through the grapevine, I understood their plea. The suave voice of the Cunning Fox quickly pierced my ears. Once again, the angry animal's looks of rage caused me a rippling fear.

"I am the King of Foxes. I represent the Prosecution. It is my pleasure to bring forth man's execution. Long have I been tired of his unscrupulous and reprehensible ways. I am proud to be the conductor to bring forth the end of his days! Since his appearance on earth, things have gone down for us all. I will take great reverence in bringing about his imminent downfall."

The old sly fox stared directly at me. Then he stated, "I call to the stand, a creature who truly despises man. For he is the last of his kind. Sir, please state your case, with moderate haste, and I'm sure a guilty verdict we can find." The Arrogant Fox chuckled as he let the monocle drop from his eye, and I thought to myself, *Boy I'd like to belt that guy.*

The agitated tiger eagerly took the stand, upset as he reminisced about the abuse his kind has received from man. "I'm the tiger from the Land Down Under, a place you call Tasmania. If you were to kill a man today, why I wouldn't blame ya, for he has done a great injustice to my tribe. Well, he hunted us, poisoned us, shot us down by the thousands, until I'm the last one alive. He wanted us out to make room for his farm and his sheep. He chased away all the food until we starved with nothing to eat. I say they die! Kill man as quickly as we can, the world would be much better off without the presence of man."

"Man's a killer!"

"He's a murderer!"

"His destructive acts can no longer be allowed!" Just a few of the unpleasing statements being yelled by the enraged animal

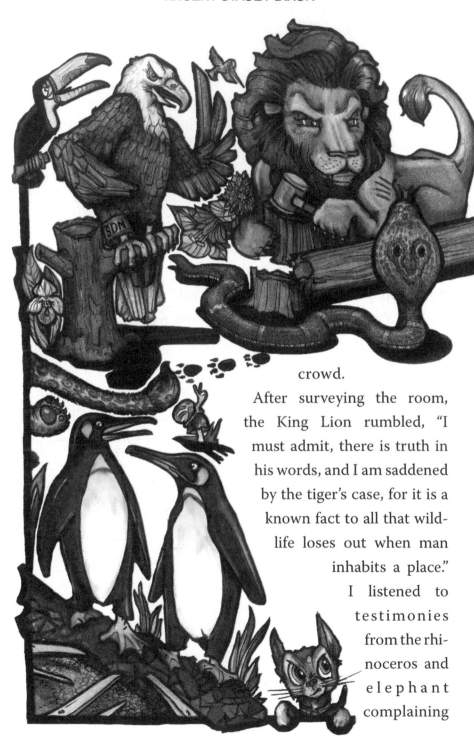

crowd.

After surveying the room, the King Lion rumbled, "I must admit, there is truth in his words, and I am saddened by the tiger's case, for it is a known fact to all that wildlife loses out when man inhabits a place."

I listened to testimonies from the rhinoceros and elephant complaining

of

l o s i n g

their tusk. No other creature on the
planet would kill just to have them,
no one, that is, but us. Many other creatures have grievances about being bred
just for food. Living conditions and
hormone manipulation, but
the animals have no
choice in man's
rules. Recalls of
chainsaws and
explosives cut-

ting down their trees and blowing up their homes, nightmarish accounts by survivors where everything was gone.

My body stiffened, on constant guard as the lion was about to break into a long-winded speech, but to everyone's surprise, a figure dropped down from the skies and out came a loud and startling screech!

"Awwwwk! I can no longer hold my tongue! I demand to be heard!" From the trees flew down the King of Parrots, a beautiful royal bird.

"I am the King of Parrots, and I speak for all of my kind. We believe that a world without man would truly be divine! For hundreds of years he has trapped us, forced us to live in cages, clipped our wings so we cannot fly, doomed to never again know the open spaces. He allows us to breed, then takes our offspring away. You can't imagine the torture day after unflying day."

"What a tragedy! What a tale!" The prosecution wailed. "I will get you that extinction verdict. I promise I will not fail! Man has toyed with us for far too long. It is time he answers for such atrocious wrongs! I vow to fight him until there is nothing of me left! Oh, what an honor to watch man put to death!" The crowd burst out in a triumphant cheer! Someone yelled out, "Never fear! Never fear! The fox is here!

"Enough! Enough!" the Great Lion roared. "I will not tolerate these kinds of outbreaks here in my court. You will all take a moment and simmer down, for only through calm debate can man's outcome be found." The fox spoke up as if he were on stage, well versed and rehearsed for a part he has often played. "I apologize, Your Honor," the fox said. "But you must understand that, I, the Red Fox, am an endangered species because of the hand of man. He hunted us with the aid of his hounds just for the sport. As I look around, how many of you can say that in this deciding court? With most of my kind, he used traps or poison, but it wasn't a merciful note. He didn't want to use a gun and risk damaging our coats!"

The prosecution went on for hours and hours, animal after animal, spewing stories of man's misuse of his powers. My heart began to sink. My head throbbed in turmoil and confusion; everything they were saying was true. Destroying the earth seemed to be man's conclusion. It seems we were given dominion over the earth, but somewhere along the way, we have forgotten that power's worth. As a fear-fueled tear makes its way down my face, for the very first time, I am terrified for the human race.

"Well, Your Honor, there you have it, we have done our best. Man can no longer go around abusing animals while sticking out his chest. Until you ask for closing arguments, the prosecution rest." The room became filled with an uneasy pause, but I tensed up even more when the Great Lion opened his jaws.

"Now we have heard so many negative things man has done—his brutal captivations, elimination of whole tribes, and possible global destruction. His wanton disregard and, in many ways, disrespect, certainly, it does not leave a pretty picture for us to reflect. Still, keep in mind you've only heard one side, and now is not the time for a judgment call. You must refrain from making a decision, until you've heard it all. We shall adjourn for today. Tomorrow, defense will have their say."

CHAPTER V

The grand doors opened, and a path of moonlight swept in. The Chimpanzee came to my side and said, "Follow me my friend." As we made our way back up the isle past the menagerie of angry beast, many started to hiss and growl, then applauded when a wolf snapped at me. Down a wooden corridor our echoing steps could be heard, moving along hurryingly, not uttering a single word. Deeper inside the fortress we walked until he pointed toward a rusty iron cage, just like the one we kept our dog spike in, until he died of ripe old age. The Chimpanzee stated that I should go inside, then he slammed the bars shut and my soul relinquished its pride. The Chimpanzee handed me a bowl of fruits and nuts. Then he gave me a small bowl of water and said, "Let this fill your gut."

He made it painfully clear that I was captive and he was free. "We are so close in character," I said. "Why do you hate me?"

"It's not that I hate you," he said with a shrug. "We get along just fine. What you do not realize is, with you out of the way, Chimpanzees are next in line."

Slowly, I made myself a bed of grass and leaves, knowing that before I could sleep tonight, I'd better get down on my knees. With my hands clutched in front of my chin, I closed my eyes, tilted my head up to the sky and began, "Now I lay me down to sleep. I pray to the Lord, Man's soul to keep. Although in the past he has destroyed the earth, help me now to find the words to explain man's worth. Save us from this untimely end. I pray for wisdom and mercy. Amen." After saying my prayers, I closed my eyes at a feeble attempt to slumber, but my mind raced one hundred miles per hour. My heart was beating louder than thunder. What would I do? What could I say? The weight of humanity was too great! With so many against us, it may already be too late. Still, there must be a solution in which we can agree upon. How strange this world would be if man were totally gone. Animals running rampant in the buildings and the streets, like tigers hiding at the top of escalators ready to pounce on something to eat. Creatures living in abandoned cars, buses and trains, as the grass and the trees and the vines of the forests engulf it all, until no sign of man remains.

As I lay there in solitude visualizing a world without man, the King of Canines walked up to my cage and placed his paw on my hand. "I too know that the monkeys are next in line. Since I don't trust them, I have decided to stay close at your side.

Right now you should rest. The defense will not have to struggle to persuade. The right choices will be made. Man realized his mistakes a long time ago; the earth just needs time to heal. The Eagle is wise; he will help them see your position, and many of your opponents will change the way they feel. There is good and bad in all of us, animal and mankind alike. When you take the stand, speak from your heart, and everything will be all right," The dog's words were soothing. They helped me to calm down. The sweet sound of the night owls hooting entertained everyone around.

I sat there watching the menagerie of animals slowly falling asleep. Every now and then each one of them would open an eye and peep. Despite all the excitement and anguish inside I felt, I realized I was very tired and began to doze myself, when the King of Cobras slithered up to me and whispered, "If you want to escape, I'll help. Mankind's fate is sealed. There is nothing more you can do. If you were to run away right now, no one would be ashamed of you. I'll tell them we spoke in the night and you felt all hope was gone. You ran away to make peace with your God. You said to let the extinction of man go on."

"Thank you, King Cobra" I said in a sarcastic way. "The way you snuck past all these animals to deliver that option was very bold. Truly you have a heart of gold. Still, I'll take my chances in court tomorrow. Let mankind's story be told." I watched as the disappointed snake slithered away as quietly as he came. Suddenly, I was invigorated. My soul regained courage and my thoughts were forever changed.

CHAPTER VI

The clean air screened sunshine through its warm breeze. Although my mind was sound and rested, I was still a little weak in the knees. Animals gathered around from all over the world: elephants, zebras, wombats, hawks, elks, canaries, and squirrels. The news traveled far and fast that man's defense was about to begin. All were curious to see, who was still man's friend? The most hunted and nearly extinct wanted to see man dead. A hand full wanted to see man suffer in shame and lose his place as the head. Still, a lot felt man had purpose and hoped to give him a second chance instead. A few of the animals like sheep, horses and cows, seemed to be undecided. Although they had been domesticated, they enjoyed the care that man provided.

Once inside, the mighty lion's eyes cast caution, and his roar stilled the air. "Today we will hear what defense has to say and listen with great concern and care. For we all know, this is not the last trial of its kind, and one day, your tribe might occupy that chair. Now let us proceed with no further wait and listen carefully to the facts the defense has to state."

Everyone watched anxiously as the Bald Eagle took his time approaching the bench. He seemed to be enjoying the stroll while keeping all of us in suspense. He paused for a moment, then looked to the sky, then spread his wings as if he were ready to fly. Finally, the great bird stopped, faced the lion, and boldly stuck out his chest as he tucked away his wings with ease and finesse. Then he proclaimed, "I head the defense, and I am here to prove that a world without man is against the greater good and not worth all we would lose. Now I know many of you hate man and would love to see him die. I am willing to admit that some of the stories from the prosecution even made me want to cry. All men are not alike, just as we are. Some are gentle and some are mad. It would not be justice if we kill the innocent simply to revenge the bad. I will now call the Hyena. Please take the stand. Tell the truth, the whole truth, and nothing but the truth of how you feel about man."

She walked over to me, looked directly in my face, and her eyes seemed to say, "I understand." Then all of a sudden, from out of nowhere, her chuckling began.

"Hahahahaha. I am the Queen of Hyenas. I would like to be the first to speak in man's behalf. When I talk, I am very serious. Hahahaha. Even though it may sound as if I laugh. Hahahaha, I do not believe our laws state the pampering of any tribe. Hahahaha. Man only lives by the very same first law: only the strong survive. Why are we so anxious. Hahahaha. To put man's life up on a shelf? Hahaha. If he has learned from his mistakes, hahaha, we will all benefit. Hahaha. If not, he will destroy himself. Hahahaha. Let man live and see what happens. Hahahaha. If he doesn't work out, we will enjoy his meat and bones on the back end. Hahahahaha." The Hyena's laughter began to fade as she rose and walked away, obviously pleased with what she had to say. Many of the animals began to shake their heads and ponder, because what the Hyena said was true. They believed our entire planet was based on natural selection. In other words, Mother Nature already knew what to do.

"So true, so true, wise Hyena Queen," the Lion Judge said. "You suggest that we let nature run its course, for like earthquakes and floods, disease and fires, man is a natural force." The crowd let out an agreeable moan that was quickly silenced by a comforting tone. "Purr! Purr!" With a soft seductive purr, the Queen of Felines arrived, sashaying her furry hips seductively from side to side, a beautiful white Persian with the purest of blue eyes. "I am here to speak. I stand with the defenses' side. My clan has been around for hundreds of years, and we inhabit all parts of the earth. We have lived with man since the beginning of his time, and understand his worth. He provides cures for illnesses that might otherwise wipe out us all. Though he has killed numerous in the past, he has also saved many tribes from a downfall. It would be such a shame to lose him just as he's getting it right. If you decide to destroy him, my clan is prepared to fight." Sounds of war filled the air as the feline revealed her claws. You see, the felines are a special breed governed by their own laws.

The Great Lion sat there quietly contemplating the feline's way of thinking, when he noticed all eyes were at the back of the court, some bucked, many squinted; others were dazed or blinking. I even strained to see what was happening at the other end of the aisle. I became stiff as my eyes focused on a large mean-looking crocodile. As the great beast made his way, I had plenty of time to wonder. Why would the crocodile speak on man's behalf when we had always dragged him under?

I had little time for a second thought, before the crocodile picked up his pace. No one had time to question his actions, for in a blink of an eye, before I could take a breath, he was standing only inches from my face! My body shuddered and shook, but still I forced calmness to my nerves. He looked as if he was going to bite my head off and say, "That's what man deserves!" Instead, he turned to the judge and said, "Your Honor, I do not wish to be rude, but it is becoming very difficult to sit among all this food. I would like to speak my mind and be quickly on my way. The truth is, I could eat any one of you on any given day. You all look quite puzzled to see me here in pro of Man, especially when we all know that he uses lizard hide to make shoes for his feet, coats for his back, and gloves to wear on his itty bitty hands. Still, none of you really like us, gators or crocs. And as far as we're concerned, Man is like the rest of you, just another herd of livestock. Yet we all survive together. We live with an uneasy peace. It's crazy to think that all your troubles would be over if Man's life were to cease. My point is parallel to the hyena's: only the strong survive. Man has proven his strength and deserves to remain alive." As the crocodile turned to walk away, he snapped at a nearby Elk. "Sorry, Your Honor, instincts you know. I just couldn't help myself." The lion paused for a moment with a frown upon his brow. The crocodile was right. This world is all about survival, and Man knew how. Whether he was right

or wrong wasn't the question here. Whether he was destroying the entire earth was the real issue, I feared. Hundreds of
animals spoke proudly in Man's behalf: Dogs, horses, owls, and
fowls, and even the king and queen of giraffes. By the time the
defense was finished, the thought of man being around wasn't

so bad. The Eagle had done his job, because many of the animals weren't so mad. "Well, Your Honor, there you have it," the Mighty Eagle said sticking out his chest. "Until the time comes for man to speak, we, of the defense, rest."

"Throughout this session, we have heard so many positive things that man is capable of: righting his wrongs, preserving the earth, and showing great animal love. This human before us has heard it all without uttering as much as a word. Soon, we will give him that same respect and a man's voice will finally be heard!" The lion's mighty frame hovered over the court as he hit the gavel on his desk. "I grow weary and desire a nap, so we will take a short recess."

CHAPTER VII

Shortly, prosecution will have their closing remarks. The old sly fox stood ready for the proceedings to start. After what seemed like an eternity, the regal old lion returned to the floor. Upon his entrance all was quiet; there was no need to roar. He pulled at his prickly whiskers, shuffled papers, and reviewed his notes. Then the lion spoke slowly after clearing his throat.

"This has been a long and demanding trial. Truly it has been a test on our nerves. All that was said was necessary for us to decide what man deserves. Prosecution may begin. Be brief and tactful with what you say. For the time is now to hear final arguments. Let us proceed with no further delay."

"There it is, Your Honor," the Sly Fox said, feeling as though he had won. "There's not much to say. To allow man to live is to sentence us to die. He won't have it any other way. We should erase man from all existence before he does the same to us. We could consult with the Golden Toad, or the Zanzibar Leopard; but because of man, they're not here to discuss. How about the

California Grizzly or the Carolina Parakeet? Maybe they have something to say. Oh, wait! They're not here either! Why? Because man snuffed their lives away." The crowd cheered as the fox walked away triumphantly. He shrugged his shoulders as he passed right in front of me. The Eagle readily approached the bench. From his strong presence, I felt a quick surge of confidence. The Eagle is wise; he knew that the end for man was absurd. He was certain to save the day by articulating just the right words. Thus, I was surprised when the powerful bird laid his wing upon my knee, turned his yellowish brown eyes in my direction and said, "It is time for you to speak. Nothing I could say right now would have any profound effect. No speech, no prayer, no valiant plea. just you and your words direct. Gather yourself together, my son. It is time to be a man. Every creature in this building is silent and listening to you. Now make them understand." Suddenly, all eyes were on me. I could tell from the unsettling looks I was getting there was a chance I might not go free. I broke out into an instant sweat. "Oh God!" Inside my head I screamed, "I'm not ready yet!"

"Well, my son!" the lion said abruptly, "what are you waiting for? Surely you've had time to prepare a speech. What you voice right now can be the deciding factor in the verdict we are about to reach."

I stood up, nervously trying to figure out where to start. I looked at the dog. He smiled at me and these words began to pour from my heart. "Although I feel unworthy to speak for all mankind, I will do so with human dignity and pride. We are a young tribe. As tribes go, yet we can adapt to any climate on earth. We are the only creature on the planet that can do that. It proves we belong here. It's the beginning of our worth. Mankind is very fragile when compared to most of you, but remember, we are all fragile at birth. We have mastered the land and seas. We have mastered the sky and seek to master space. I admit a lot of us lose respect for our surroundings no matter where the place. We cannot correct many of our past mistakes, and for this, I truly apologize. Many have learned to take care of our planet now, for you see, time has opened our eyes. To those of you who would have us condemned, I regret your suffering and pain. I will gladly give my life as payment if you will allow mankind to remain. There are millions who work hard every day to help all animals survive, and I'm sure when word of this trial gets out, it will open even more eyes. So in closing, I'd like to say, please, please give us a chance. We won't let you down. If we work together, animal and mankind alike, we can keep our Mother Earth safe and sound." I watched as many of the animals nodded in approval and still heard quite a few more mumbling, still seeking mankind's removal. I felt I could convince the doubters if I could just finish my speech. So quickly I said, "This trial! This trial has made me aware of the lessons I need to learn, and if I am spared, those I am now compelled to teach. For a moment, it were as if all sound had been siphoned from the room. My shadow silhouetted in front of me as the reflection of the sun casted off the moon. The lion embarked to speak in a deep philosophic tone, as he gently tapped the wood with his heavy gavel stone. "We have heard from prosecution, from Man and his defense. Now we will adjourn so deliberations can commence. We will think about it and take our votes. May mercy guide our hearts and wisdom reside in our hopes."

CHAPTER VII

All the kings and queens gathered in the Great Hall. This was the moment of truth, would man rise or fall? It was the job of the Chipmunk Army to collect up all the votes, bring them to the Baboon Brigade, who would count them and deliver the quote. Surprisingly little time had elapsed before all the royalty rejoined the room. Some looked quite happy; others seemed fearful of doom. The Titanic Lion roared and tilted his beastly head. "Man will rise and stand before me so that his verdict can be read. It is not my desire to keep this court in suspense, but I feel I must say these words. The decision reached by the kings and queens today was based purely on what they have heard. It is true that no animal has the right to take Man's life into his own hooves, wings, or claws, but for the first time in history, Man will have to abide by the animal's laws. We are stilled by your emotions, awed by your offer of sacrifice. But no one should die needlessly. We should all have respect for life. Deliverer of the verdict, please stand and read the outcome aloud." And as the Mandrill stood up, there were no peeps or

hoots or snarls or growls. Not a single sound from the animal crowd. Then the red-and-blue nosed Mandrill spoke, "After much deliberation, the Animal Kingdom has reached a decision. We feel that man has not been true to or fair to animals, himself, or his religion. Arrogant! Belligerent! Living with man is becoming increasingly hard. Therefore, we find Man guilty! Guilty as charged! He is guilty of inhumane acts, cruelty to animals, and total destruction at large!" The air exploded with animal sounds! Some so loud that it shook the ground. The lion slammed his gavel in an attempt to regain order in his court, but so many animals were crying, while others were celebrating, and others yelled the news as they ran from the fort.

"Wait! Wait!" the angry lion shouted. "I am seeing a contingency clause here. The judgment also decided to show Man some leniency, so his sentence won't be carried out for a period of one year. During this time Man's thinking must change and you are the key. You will speak for all animal kind against the scourge of humanity." The lion turned and looked at me as he spread his claws. I became terrified as saliva began to moisten his jaws. "Go tell them we will not take abuse anymore. We animals have rights that can no longer be ignored. You humans have called for the abolishment of all Man's slavery, but still confine animals to cages. That's what enrages me! Warn your people, do the best that you can. You are the last hope for the salvation of Man. "Humanity will be given one last try. If Man does not adhere to our rights, then in one year from today, you will all begin to die! Now, unless there is something we have missed... I now declare this court dismissed."

Animals began making noises that could be heard from miles around, expressing pain and anger, spreading the news with the most alarming of sounds. My defense moved toward me rather quickly. They snatched me up fast as the Bear yelled, "Come on, boy! Stick with me! The Dog and the Bear escorted me rapidly through a secret door in the rear of the lion's chamber den. I felt as we began to run, if I did not clear the woods, my life would come to an end. The Dog and the Bear yelled, "Hurry, boy, you must make it through that gate! We'll hold them off as long as we can, but you must escape!" I could hear the other creatures hissing and growling, full of animal rage. Then I heard the fox yell, "There he is! There he is! Someone get the cage!" I continued running through the thickets as fast as I could. I had to get out of these woods! Thorns tore into my legs, branches slapping me repeatedly in the eyes. Finally, I fell through a clearing, and there stood my father to my surprise! I tried to hide the look of panic written all over my face and cleared my head just in time to hear him say. "Hey, boy, what happened to you? We've been looking for you for days! Most folks had given up, figured you'd passed away. Where's my gun? The fur and the food? Why do you look so beat up and hazy? What's going on with you?" As I lay there reeling in pain from the thorns and possibly barbed wire, I said, "Daddy, tonight let's just break bread. There's a story I'd like to tell you by the fire." My dad agreed with a reluctant smile and reached out his hand. It was at that moment when I stood up, and I knew this boy was now a man. He sent me to hunt for meat to go with mama's bread, but Daddy I'm coming home with a greater message instead.

CHAPTER VIII

The night unleashed frigid misty air that was partnered by the moonlight, as lightning bugs flew in clusters all about. A giant bullfrog sits in the creek, in solitude croaking out. The animals rescinded back into the woods, some egos bruised, no doubt.

I could hear the night owls calling out, but they were hooting a different sound. I knew that they were delivering the news of Man's trial to all the nocturnal creatures around. This was a defining moment meant to be shared throughout the land. A ruling had been made in the trial of man.

I sat by the fireplace wrapped up in a blanket, thinking of all that had just happened to me. How I set out to prove myself to be a great hunter and instead I came back in defeat. Captured and put on trial, something that has never been done to man before. Now I am faced with the burden of changing the world before the animals even the score. Relieved that I was finally back at home after being gone for well over a week. My father, mother, and the kids were all tired from being out there looking for me. Mom suggested that we all go to bed, and my father agreed with a nod of his head. *I will explain everything in the morning,* I thought to myself, *and be as detailed as I can.* I know then that my father will help me, on my crusade for the salvation of Man.

I will tell him how I met the Bear in the woods and all about the abandoned fort. I'll describe the Mighty Lion Judge and all the animals in court. I will tell him about the prosecuting Fox who stayed angry all the time. Of course, I'll mention the King Cobra who tried to get inside my mind. I won't forget to talk about the Great Bald Eagle who brilliantly led my defense or the sensible crocodile that kept the entire courtroom in suspense. I will lay out all the animal's grievances, from the big to the small. Get everyone around to listen to me, at a meeting we'll set up in the town hall. As I sat there listening to the crackle of the wood and the fire warming my face, I had no idea that deep within the forest an ominous conversation was taking place.

"The trial was not fair! The mercy clause should not have been included! I believe that man should die now, just as you did. But the laws have been set. There's nothing we can do now." Then a familiar voice hissed in a slow angry growl, "Who cares about their laws and that silly trial. Man can still be eliminated, and I know just how. But for my plan to work we'll have to move fast. This kind of undertaking will not be an easy task. First thing we need to find out is, how many are in that house, and I will get that information from the scared little mouse. Next, we find a way to eliminate them all, sealing Man's fate and guaranteeing his downfall."

Then the strange voice that was lurking in the shadows, never showing his face, said, "How will killing all of them dispose of the human race?"

The snake replied, "The trial was only yesterday. He hasn't had a chance to tell anyone else. But I am sure he will tell his family now or in the morning that much can't be helped. If we can eliminate them all, before they can pass along the word. Then for humans the trial of mankind will never be heard. Without that knowledge, they won't seek change and will continue to destroy with disperse." Then the stranger interrupted. "And without that change, one year from today, man will lose his worth! It will be a moment I will always cherish, because then, we will take over the earth. It must look like a series of accidents so the other animals won't know. Otherwise, they may condemn us both and their bond with man will grow." The two evil creatures spoke well into the night as plans were made for what they professed to do. Then they sought help from some of the other animals that still despised man and wanted to see him eliminated too.

By this time, the sun was rising and the Rooster began to crow. Its warmth brought on a calming feeling as its light made the morning dew in the grass glow. The air was crisp and clean, the sky a solid blue. Aromas of Honeysuckle awakened the senses as it began to fill the room. We all sat down to breakfast. I was silent as mama made my plate. We all had scrambled eggs and sausage with those buttery light biscuits she liked to bake. My father said abruptly, "So get on with it, boy. What is it you have to say? I got a lot of chores to do, and I still have to go hunting today. You didn't come back with any food or any fur and you lost my gun. Right now I hate to say it, but I am ashamed to call you my son."

"Now, Papa!" my mother snapped. "That's not nice and you're not being fair. You have always trusted in that boy, or you wouldn't have let him go out there. Let's hear what he's got to say before you get all upset. I'm sure whatever it is has got him filled with just as much regret."

I began by talking about the kindly old bear I met on the path, when I noticed my siblings were giggling. And as I continued, they started to laugh. "Hush," my mother whispered through her own grin. "Let's just hear your brother out. You both be quiet until the end." When I was done telling my amazing tale, I was surprised by my father who began to yell, "Boy, you must be out of your mind to come in here and give me that crazy report. About talking Bears and Lions and snakes and being put to trial in court. What is this all about, this trial of mankind, and people changing their ways?" My dad stood up and started pacing back and forth as he continued his rave. "I believe you just ate the wrong berries and passed out as they put your mind in a daze. I think somebody came along, stole the gun, and left you there for dead. So when you came to, you realized your shame and made up this insane story instead."

"That's not true!" I barked back. "Everything I told you is right. If we don't get this message out that people have to change the way they think, a year from today, the animals will strike! They're tired of being mistreated, sick of the abuse. They understand the rules of hunting, but not the heartless experimental use. Some willingly admit that we belong because only the strong survive. The problem with that is, man tends to overdo it and wipe out entire tribes."

"OK! Enough!" My papa barked back. "Just don't say anymore. All of this sounds like nonsense, like nothing I've ever heard before. And for your information! If the animals did want to fight, I would gladly give them war!" As he stormed out and slammed the door, the picture of him and his father hunting came crashing to the floor. I looked out the window to see him stomp off, but he stopped at the edge of the porch stairs, then he carefully staggered back with his head in his hands and flopped down in one of the rocking chairs.

My father's words continued echoing inside my head, as well as those of the mighty lion who instructed me just before

I fled. My mind began swimming as my thoughts conjured the realization of animal and man at war. Who would win? Who would lose? And who would be keeping score? What if all the insects in the world banded together to sabotage the fields and crops? Or the great herds of the world flooded into our cities, causing all traffic to stop. Fish clogging up our water filtration systems, making it hard for man to drink. Whales and sharks and all manner of marine life attacking boats until each one of them sinks. Birds sacrificing themselves to jet engines to keep man out of the skies. All animals and creatures functioning on one accord, with one thought—man dies!

The humans will fight back with all types of guns and knives. They are the masters of technology and will use various forms of pesticides. Horrific sights of death and destruction would be seen by everyone's eyes. In the end, no one would win, and no one would be left to call it a tie. My nightmarish vision was interrupted by the sounds of my younger sister and brother; they were about to go outside along with my mother. "I'm going to talk to your father," she said ever so softly. "Get him to calm down. While these two check in the nearby woods to see if his gun can be found. What you're saying is really hard to take in that's why your father is making such a fuss. You've never given us any reason not to believe in you, so when you say that's what happened, that's what I trust. Your father, on the other hand, won't be that easy. For him you're going to need some kind of proof. Maybe you can get one of your animal friends to come by and speak up for you." I didn't know whether she was being sarcastic or offering me support. Before I could question her ambiguous statement, she was completely out the door.

Just then at the edge of the woods, the king cobra stuck his head above the tall grass. "Come here! Come here! Come here, my friends," he hissed. "An opportunity at last! I see the younger siblings heading off into the woods. How sad it would be for them to have an accident, but for us that would be really good."

"I will create a distraction" the old sly fox said. For you see he had joined their nefarious plans. "I'll get the attention of the woman and the man. This will give you time for whatever you need to. You see nothing makes more noise than a fox in a chicken coop!" The fox made his way over to the edge of the fence. He jumped inside the coop and the ruckus immediately commenced. The chickens started cackling in panic. There were feathers flying everywhere. My mother turned and ran in the direction of the disturbance and so did my father as he bolted out of the chair. They both got there just in time to chase the mean Old Fox away. Then began checking the chickens to make sure they were all OK. My papa said angrily, "I'm going after that fox just as soon as I get my spare rifle. You go back around front and gather the kids. That unnerved me just a trifle."

Mama obeyed without saying a word. She quickly ran back around front to get the young pair. Her heart was filled with immediate panic when she didn't see them anywhere. She stopped and listened for any sound they could make. Like laughter from playing, or running, which would cause the twigs to break. She heard nothing and became quickly consumed with what every mother feared: two of her children had actually disappeared! She ran in the direction where she last saw them. Eventually running into some scraps of their clothes leading up to an empty well. It looked as though they had both fallen in, but it was too dark and deep to tell. Mama hollered inside and listened for their call. She became afraid they may have been knocked unconscious from the distance of the fall.

"Hahaha. Hmmhmmm." From far on the other side of the forest, the strange voice grumbled with joy. "My sources tell me the younglings are gone. That leaves the mother, father, and the boy."

"The mother is distraught." the evil snake said. "She believes her children fell down the well. But I saw the tiger from Tasmania tracking them by smell." The strange voice noted. "The mother will undoubtedly go back to the house for help" The snake hissed. "I'll have someone intercept her, then we attack the father. But I want the boy to myself! I have tried to help him, and he has turned me down twice. Now I must make him sorry. He didn't heed my advice. Then I will take him up on his offer of sacrifice!" The air was thick with evil thoughts and laughter as the two conniving beast departed, confident in their plans that the end of man had truly started.

CHAPTER IX

I have been sitting here all morning, trying to figure out what went wrong. What happened to unwind this father-and-son bond that used to be so strong? I know I went out hunting and came back empty-handed. So I didn't face the challenges that our lifestyle demanded. To top it all off, I lost his favorite gun. I know he's somewhere hurting, brooding, and thinking, and asking, "Why did it have to be my son? If the animals did talk." He'd be saying through his tears. "They should have come after me I've been hunting them for years."

"Well, I don't know why they chose me." I'm reflecting as I stand. "Enough contemplating, it's time to face this insanity! It's time for me to be a man."

I stepped out on the porch and swiftly looked around, but everyone was gone. Suspicion overtook me, and I felt something was going on. Mama and Papa would not have taken the kids and left without telling me. My eyes focused on signs around the yard that piqued my curiosity. No bees in the flowers. The yard void of chickens running around, not even sheep bleating in the field, which was a common everyday sound.

Ripples in the wind snapped up my senses, and I perceived something was wrong. Especially when I didn't hear mama humming or singing a song. It felt as though all the animals around were silent, waiting to see what I was going to do, but everything that had recently transpired, I didn't have a clue.

Although I didn't know it at the time, Mama was running back to the house as fast as she could from the well to get help and some rope. She found herself being surrounded by a herd of sheep who engulfed her body in their wooly coats. Though struggling with all her might, they had her under full restraint. Petrified with fear, my mother would soon faint. News spread fast that she was down. Rumor was she got accidently trampled to the ground.

"Have you heard the news?" the strange voice said. "Those sheep have done our dirty work for us! What a stroke of luck. Now you can go after the boy, while the father is being lured by the fox. Our plan is working perfectly. We're already in the final phase. I'm beginning to see the future where the world of man decays. No longer will we be subject to his unjust rules, the earth will be forever changed when we eliminate these fools. None of this would be possible," he said, praising the snake. "Without you on board. And as promised, you can have the boy as your reward. Before you go, I need a minute of your time. There is something else you must do for me. It's all about tying up loose ends, and this one is important, you'll see." Tracking the fox, my papa had traveled well over a mile. He was determined to capture him and prove that he was still King of the Wild. "How dare

they attack my son, he said they threw him in a cage. He told me a fox was the prosecutor! Well, I'm not going to let this one get away!" He pressed on with dominance and thoughts like that to fuel his hunting rage. Every now and then the foxe's bushy tail would stick out and my father would take a shot. But that Sly Fox knew exactly when to move and when to duck; he wasn't about to get caught. In fact, he was leading my father straight into a trap. One that had been set up earlier by the snake who had showed the fox a map. One giant leap in the air, my papa shot, and the fox screamed out! "Got him!" my father yelled "That's what I'm talking about!" He cautiously moved closer to the sounds of the fox rustling and whimpering as he

53

was lying on the ground. Suddenly, a snapping of twigs, the rifle slipped out of his hand, and my papa was falling down. He hit the dirt so hard that it raised a cloud of dust. The fox peeked over the side, smiled, and said, "The hunter has become the hunted. Now what do you think of us?"

Dazed and confused, my father looked up as he wiped the dirt from his eyes. He realized the fox was talking to him and was utterly, completely surprised. "So you can talk," he said with amazement. "My son was telling the truth."

"Yea, what of it?" the fox growled back. "That's irrelevant compared to what's about to happen to you. Without that rifle, you're not so tough. I could jump down there right now and ruffle you up! You will no longer hunt and kill my friends. Now it is time for my revenge!" *Swoosh!* Without warning, there came a loud thwack! As something hard and scaly struck the fox in the back.

He tumbled over and fell into the hole. Then a strange voice called out, "Pardon me for being so bold." The fox shook it off and blurted, "You've trapped me down here now, and I want to know why?" The mysterious voice answered, "In order for my plan to work, both of you must go bye-bye! With the knowledge you both have there is an acquired risk. That one of you may live and expose all of this. As I told the snake, when I killed and swallowed him in, I don't like to leave any loose ends. Taking  you both out will fill that void, then the only one left will be the boy. You will undoubtedly attack each other until one of you dies, then I will come back and kill the one that survives." As the shadow began to fill the hole, the fox recognized the smile. He and my father both gasped with shock to see the face of the crocodile!

"We have existed since the dawn of dinosaurs. We have lived through over a million years of wars. We could never seek a friendship with either side. Animals fear and hate us. Man values our hide. Your kinds will destroy each other, and the earth will once again know peace. Then the crocodiles and alligators and lizards of the world will all enjoy a mighty feast." The crocodile added a naughty laugh as he turned away. "I'll be back soon."

His eyes squinted. "You both enjoy the rest of your day."

It was midafternoon, and the sun was beaming down hot. I could see heat waves rising up, and I was sweating a lot. Looking around in all directions, it was just as I had feared. My family has disappeared. As I combed the woods with fearful eyes, I am trying not to think the worse, then I noticed a five-point buck, and dangling from his antlers was a piece of my mother's skirt.

"Hey! Mr. Buck!" I hollered. "I need to talk to you! What happened to my family? What did you do?" The Buck turned and started trotting without saying a word to me. I took out after him; I needed some answers about where my family could be. I was getting angry. It was hard to keep up, running and yelling at the same time. Then I began to realize that old Buck never let me get too far behind. We walked up and down hill and dale, and it seemed like we were going in circles at times. I thought he was trying to confuse me, another attempt to obscure my mind. Then he stopped and scratched at the ground, bobbed his head and began to snort. I immediately recognized my surroundings; I was back at the abandoned fort. Once again, I walked down the familiar gray hall toward the stellar bronze doors. But when they swung open, I gasped as I saw my brother and sister playing on the floor. They were tossing a ball with a couple of ferrets just having a good old time. When they saw me, their faces lit up with a radiant shine. Then they simultaneously yelled, "We're so glad you weren't lying!" Then I heard my mama sound out in laughter. "Hahaha, Mister Chimpanzee, you have got a date, and the first thing I'm going to do when I get home is bake you a great big banana cream cake."

"Mama, mama," I shouted with joy. "I'm so glad to see you're all right! I was petrified beyond fear when I came outside and my family had vanished from clear sight. I thought something really awful had happened. You couldn't imagine what I visualized!" I grabbed her and hugged real tight, but like a man, I held back the tears in my eyes. "I must admit I'm at a loss for words," I said. "How did you all get here?"

"That would be my doing," a familiar authoritative voice revealed. "But they had to disappear." It was the Mighty Lion Judge coming out of a room. "I got news from a tiny little mouse that your family might be facing doom. He said the King Cobra paid him a visit and demanded to know how many lived inside. The mouse promised to tell him if he let him go, and as he made his escape, he yelled five. That brave little mouse made his way here and told me everything that had just taken place. Then I had your family secretly brought to the fort where we know they would be safe. I had the dog and the cat gather up your brother and sister and leave bits of clothing leading up to the well. When your mother saw this, her grief was authentic so the other animals couldn't tell. Then I had her abducted by a large herd of sheep. News spread of her fatal accident, and they carried her here with discreet. I was going after your father, but he was busy chasing the fox. They were last seen running into the swamps where humans are usually eaten by crocs."

The atmosphere in the swamp is tense; it offers no comforts of any kind. It's either kill or be killed or hunt while being hunted. One must stay on guard at all times. At the edge of the bog, there was a very large hole meant as an animal trap. But the animals learned how to use it and set the trap up for the man. The animals had also learned how to adapt.

The clay sides were too steep and wet to climb, the ground hard, dusty and cold. At this very moment, a fox and man where squaring off inside, each seeking redemption as their goal.

"Never thought I would be talking to a fox," my father said. "I'd rather be wearing you for a hat."

"I've often wondered what humans taste like," the fox replied. "The crocodiles say you're full of fat. So are we going to go back and forth and insult each other? Or are we going to fight?"

"Well, the way I see it," my dad answered, "if we don't work together, we'll both die tonight. Neither one of us is going to go down with a breeze. That means, the winner will be so tired that the crocodile will come down and defeat him with ease."

"So what do you propose we do?" the fox inquired. "It will be hard to work together when I don't trust you."

My father said abruptly, "For my plan to work, you don't have to."

The crocodile had been basking in the sun building up his grit, preparing himself for a battle with the winner between the fox and the man in the pit. He made his way back to the hole and peeped in with one eye. He saw the man sitting there covered in blood and the fox lay lifeless at his side. This is his time to strike; man is too tired to run. He will be the superior force since the human has no knife or gun. He crept his way down through a secret tunnel then busted in through the sidewall dirt. He screamed, "Die, human!" and lunged at my father with all his length and girth.

My father jumped up and rolled out the way, landing on his feet with a long tree root vine in his hand. He yelled, "I have killed the fox! Now I'm ready for you! Come on, Crocodile, let's dance!" Both figures moved in a circle with slow intensity, waiting for an opening to strike, or for the other to attack. When a curdling growl came arching through the air and the fox landed on the crocodiles back! The Croc was caught off guard, and when he turned, my father jumped on him and wrapped the root vine around his mouth. The fox was biting his tail while being thrashed around as my father was tying a knot around his snout. There was so much growling and yelling; it sounded like a full-fledged war. Each creature fighting for their life, at that moment, their life and nothing more. When the dust settled down, the giant Croc lay on the ground exhausted and defeated; his fiendish plan had failed. The fox and my father breathing hard sitting next to each other. My dad smiling, the fox wagging his tail. "Seems to me," the fox said through his gasping breaths, "that there may be room for us both after all. That little ruse of yours saved our lives. That was a very good call. But how did you know I wouldn't try to kill you when you allowed me to scar you up? I could have clawed at your heart, scratched out your eyes; I could have made things for you really tough."

My father replied, "After all that man has put you through, I felt like you deserved that chance. In fact, after being hunted and trapped myself, I fully understand. I wondered if when the Croc was down, where you and I still going to fight?"

Then the fox interrupted, "You know what, my friend, I think there's been enough excitement for one night." My father and the fox had made their way out through the secret tunnel, and we were all safe and sound back at the fort. As we were saying our final good-byes, the animals were about to hold court. I heard the gavel slam and the lion roar. Once again, everything got quiet on the courtroom floor. "Here ye! Here ye! Court is now in session. We are here to discuss the crocodile's transgressions" As the bronze doors were closing in front of me, I realized I had no choice. I quickly jumped between them before they could slam shut and yelled, "I will be his voice!"

THE END

"I will be his voice!"

ABOUT THE AUTHOR

Vincent Stacey Dixon was born in Cleveland, Ohio, on February 5, 1961. He's the author of *The Trial of Mankind*—a novel that Vincent also performs live using his one-man visual and audio platform to characterize each person and animal's distinctive voice and demeanor. Mr. Dixon also authors the novels *Killer by Proxy* and *The Story of Parker Sway*. As a playwright, he penned "The Immaculate Conversation," revealing a new perspective on getting in touch with one's self. "The Immaculate Conversation" was performed at the Ensemble Theatre Festival in February of 2016. He is the composer of the plays "David and the Stones," (which also doubles as a musical) and "Glass Clouds," a riveting drama about the effects of drugs on an unsuspecting family. Vincent is a songwriter, bass, and baritone singer for the vocal group Sweeteven. You can find his songs on both of their CDs entitled "Sweeteven/Fellas" and "Sweeteven/Jackpot" (You've Got Love).

Scott Nylund is a forty-year-old fashion designer and illustrator living and working in New York City, NY. Nylund was born in Minneapolis, MN and raised in Owatonna, MN. In 1999, Nylund graduated from Luther College in Decorah, IA with a degree in Art. In the fall of 1999, Nylund entered the Associates program at F.I.T. in New York, and graduated in 2000 with a degree in Fashion Design.

Nylund has been sketching and designing clothing since he was in middle school when he would sketch fifty different women, each in a different gown, that represented each of the states, as if to create his own "Miss USA" pageant. Through the years his illustrations and the intricacy in his sketches has evolved to be the fully detailed and colored illustrations you see today.

In May 2009, Scott Nylund was accepted as a member of the exclusive and renowned "Society of Illustrators" in New York City.

Nylund worked on the teams for Ralph Lauren, Tommy Hilfiger and JLo by Jennifer Lopez before getting a call from a representative for Tina Knowles, the mother of Beyoncé Knowles, to interview for a chance to help launch their clothing line; House of Dereon. Upon meeting Ms. Knowles, they immediately connected and Nylund illustrated the first collections for their brands. Over the years his role was promoted to Design

Director of Beyond Productions, where he held the responsibility of directing all three of the Knowles' lines; House of Dereon, Dereon, and Miss Tina by Tina Knowles. During these years, Nylund worked closely with Miss Tina and played a major role in the design of many of Beyoncé's stage, red carpet, and video wardrobe. Most notable is the House of Dereon gown that Beyoncé wore to the Academy Awards.

Beyond Productions closed its doors in 2013, two weeks later, Nylund was offered the Design Director position at Beyoncé's new management company; Parkwood Productions. In February 2014, upon the completion of Beyoncé's self-titled album, Nylund parted ways with Parkwood and the Knowles' family.

During the last three years of exploring and spreading awareness about the South American Amazon Rainforest, Nylund has also taught and mentored at Parsons New School and the Fashion Institute of technology in NYC.

Michael R Jones is recognized as the Founder and Owner of the Entertainment media production company known as Fl@out Productions and Co-creator of the popular clothing apparel line known as MartianMovement. He has recently partnered with author Mr. Vincent Dixon to help create a unique vision on a series of media projects and novels beginning with "The Trial of Mankind."

Myron Lavell Avant, Born: April 26, 1976, better known as Avant, is an American R&B singer and songwriter. He is best known for hits such as "Separated", My First Love and "Read Your Mind". Avant has recently partnered up with Author Vincent Dixon and Fl@out Productions Owner Michael R Jones to add a unique vision to the popular Novel known as "The Trial of Mankind."

CPSIA information can be obtained
at www.ICGtesting.com
Printed in the USA
LVOW05s0427160917
548553LV00007B/19/P